MR. GOOD

Roger Hargreaves

Written and illustrated by
Adam Hargreaves

EGMONT

Mr Good is very good.

He always makes his bed.

He always cleans his teeth.

And he always wipes his feet.

He never slams doors.

He never forgets birthdays.

And he never, ever tells lies.

Mr Good is very, very good.

However, Mr Good lives in a place called Badland.

A place where nobody is like Mr Good.

A place where people do slam doors.

And they slam them in your face!

In Badland, the puddles are much deeper than they look.

In Badland, a dog's bite is worse than its bark.

In Badland, even the trees are bad!

One day, it was wet and windy.

Well, of course it was.

The weather is always bad in Badland.

Mr Good was walking along, minding his own business, when the hat of the man in front blew off.

Mr Good leapt in the air, and caught it for him.

The man turned round, and glared at Mr Good.

"What do you think you're doing?" he thundered. "Give my hat back!"

Poor Mr Good.

This sort of thing was always happening to him.

You see, the very idea of doing a good deed in Badland was preposterous, unthinkable, mad.

If Mr Good offered to help carry shopping, he was accused of stealing.

If he kindly held a door open for somebody,
then he would be kicked in the shin!

Not surprisingly, Mr Good was not very happy.

In fact he was miserable.

So he decided to go for a long walk to think about things.

He walked for a very long time.

He was so deep in thought that he did not notice how far he had gone.

And he was so deep in thought that he accidentally walked slap bang into somebody.

"Oh … oh … I … I … I'm s-s-so s-s-sorry," stammered Mr Good, nervously.

"That's quite all right," said the man, and carried on his way.

"Quite all right," repeated Mr Good to himself. "That's quite all right?"

In the whole of his life nobody had ever said "That's quite all right" to Mr Good.

Then Mr Good noticed that the sun was shining.

Which was strange, because the sun never shone in Badland.

Further on, Mr Good found a dustbin on its side.

Without thinking, he tidied up all the rubbish.

"Thank you," said a woman.

Mr Good stared at her.

In the whole of his life nobody had ever said "Thank you" to him.

"Could you tell me where I am?" he asked.

"You're in Goodland," replied the woman.

"Thank you," said Mr Good.

"My pleasure," said the woman.

Mr Good beamed.

And I am sure you have guessed that Mr Good now lives in Goodland.

And Mr Good is happy.

Very, very happy, doing good deeds all day long.

The only thing Mr Good still does not trust
are puddles.

Once you have stepped in a Badland puddle, you never forget!

Fantastic offers for Mr. Men fans!

1 MR. MEN TOKEN

Collect all your Mr. Men or Little Miss books in these superb durable collector's cases!

Only £5.99 inc. postage and packaging, these wipe clean, hard wearing cases will give all your Mr. Men and Little Miss books a beautiful new home!

Keep track of your favourite Mr. Men and Little Miss characters with this brilliant collector's poster, now featuring Mr. Nobody!

Collect 6 tokens and we will send you a giant-sized double-sided poster! Simply tape a £1 coin in the space provided and fill out the form overleaf.

Only need a few Mr. Men or Little Miss to complete your set? You can order any of the titles on the back of the books from our Mr. Men order line on 0870 787 1724. The majority of orders are delivered in 5 to 7 working days.

TO BE COMPLETED BY AN ADULT

To apply for any of these great offers, ask an adult to complete the details below and send this whole page with the appropriate payment and tokens, to: MR. MEN CLASSIC OFFER PO BOX 715, HORSHAM RH12 5WG

☐ Please send me a giant-sized double-sided collector's poster.

AND ☐ I enclose 6 tokens and have taped a £1 coin to the other side of this page

☐ Please send me ☐ Mr. Men Library case(s) and/or ☐ Little Miss Library case(s) at £5.99 each inc P&P

☐ I enclose a cheque/postal order payable to Egmont UK Limited for £.............................

OR ☐ Please debit my MasterCard / Visa / Maestro / Delta account (delete as appropriate) for £.............................

Card no. ☐☐☐☐ ☐☐☐☐ ☐☐☐☐ ☐☐☐☐ ☐☐☐☐   Security code ☐☐☐

Issue no. (if available) ☐   Start Date ☐☐ / ☐☐ / ☐☐   Expiry Date ☐☐ / ☐☐ / ☐☐

Fan's name: ....   Date of birth: ....

Address: ....

....

Postcode: ....

Name of parent / guardian: ....

Email of parent / guardian: ....

Signature of parent / guardian ....

Offer is only available while stocks last. We reserve the right to change the terms of this offer at any time and we offer a 14 day money back guarantee. Please allow up to 28 days for delivery. This does not affect your statutory rights. Offers apply to UK only.

☐ We may occasionally wish to send you information about other Egmont books. If you would rather we didn't please tick this box.